Santa's Gift to Tyler

BONNIE KRUM

ILLUSTRATED BY DEBORA ROBERTS

PAGE PUBLISHING, INC.
Conneaut Lake, PA

First originally published by Page Publishing 2021

ISBN 978-1-6624-7674-7 (pbk)
ISBN 978-1-6624-7675-4 (digital)

Printed in the United States of America

This book is dedicated to Jean Compton

It was two weeks before Christmas and all the elves were busy getting the toys ready for Santa.

Zachary was busy painting wagons red. Dover was busy making sure the dolls eyes opened and shut and Stewy was busy testing robots.

Everyone had something special to do, even Tyler. Tyler loved his job. He liked working with the play telephones. His job was to make them ring. Sometimes he pretended to call people himself. He especially liked to pretend to call his mother and say hello.

Christmas was always a hectic time of year, but all the elves enjoyed it. Mr. and Mrs. Claus made daily rounds to see that all the elves were happy and doing their work.

8

Mrs. Claus noticed during her rounds one day that one little elf seemed to be happy, but in his eyes, she could see he was sad. She mentioned it to Santa several times. Santa ho, ho, ho'd, and remarked the elf was probably just tired. There was much to do and so little time. Mrs. Claus knew in her heart something was wrong. She decided to keep an eye on Tyler. Mrs. Claus watched as Tyler did his work. While all the other elves sang songs and whistled happy tunes, Tyler worked silently. She watched at dinner time and noticed Tyler hardly ate a thing on his small plate. Mrs. Claus decided to find out what was troubling Tyler.

Three days before Christmas, while Santa slept, Mrs. Claus crept into Tyler's small room. She was surprised to hear him weeping softly. She walked softly across the floor and knelt down by his bed. She gently asked Tyler why he cried so. Tyler wiped his tears with the tissue Mrs. Claus handed him. "I don't mean to cry," whispered Tyler.

13

I am very happy here actually. I love my work and the other elves, and Santa and you are so good to me," he explained. "It's just that I always wanted a real Mom of my own," sighed Tyler. "I always dreamed of being someone's little boy." "Why, you're my little boy," replied Mrs. Claus. "I know," whimpered Tyler, but you have so many. I mean, I love you, but I want to be just one little boy for just one lonely Mom." "I understand," said Mrs. Claus.

The next morning, Mrs. Claus told Santa about Tyler. Santa, too, understood. All his elves were very special to him and he tried to give them lots of love, but with so many, it was easy to understand why Tyler might wish to have a smaller family. Then he remembered a letter he received from Mrs. Appleton. She was an older woman with no family. She wrote Santa several months ago asking him for someone to love. Her letter was so warm and caring that it touched Santa's heart. Santa was going to give her a special puppy, but now he thought differently.

17

On Christmas eve, Santa asked Tyler to ride with him on his sleigh. All the elves were surprised as Santa usually traveled alone. Tyler was most surprised of all. Mrs. Claus took off Tyler's green elf suit and put some new clothes on him. Brown slacks, blue shirt, and sweater to match, grey socks, and brown loafers made Tyler look like a small boy rather than one of Santa's elves. She also gave him a brown coat and hat to keep warm.

It was past three in the morning by the time Santa finished his Christmas deliveries. He was proud of himself as he finished this year ahead of schedule. Fortunately for him there was only a light snow falling and all of his reindeer were in top-notch condition. Rudolph did a splendid job once again of guiding his sleigh through the winter darkness. There was only one more stop to make before heading back to the North Pole. Santa pulled on the reins and the reindeer turned towards Mrs. Appleton's rooftop.

Tyler was just drifting off to sleep when Santa twitched his nose and transported Tyler and himself to Mrs. Appleton's living room. Santa laid Tyler on the couch by the Christmas tree and wrote Mrs. Appleton a note while Tyler slept. He told her Tyler was a special boy who needed lots of love and he was sure Mrs. Appleton could give it to him. He signed it, "Merry Christmas from Santa." And then with a twinkle in his eye, he kissed Tyler goodbye.

Christmas morning finally arrived. All the boys and girls were busy opening packages and enjoying the magic of Christmas. But the best magic of all was when Mrs. Appleton and Tyler realized their gift from Santa was each other and they hugged for the first time. For it's not toys that make Christmas, but the love that people share in their hearts.

24

About the Author

Bonnie Krum, a Maryland native, has been an early childhood educator for 30 years. Her works, including poetry and educational stories, have been published in local newspapers and magazines. Inspired by her four grandchildren and young students, her children's books aim to bring to life the lessons that showcase family relationships and peer-to-peer interactions.

CPSIA information can be obtained
at www.ICGtesting.com
Printed in the USA
LVRC090038291221
707430LV00003B/44